# GAME ON!

# DRIVE TO THE HOOP

BY BRANDON TERRELL

STORY LIBRARY

**www.12StoryLibrary.com**

Copyright © 2015 by Peterson Publishing Company, North Mankato, MN 56003. All rights reserved. No part of this book may be reproduced or utilized in any form or by any means without written permission from the publisher.

12-Story Library is an imprint of Peterson Publishing Company and Press Room Editions.

Produced for 12-Story Library by Red Line Editorial

Photographs ©: Shutterstock Images, cover

Cover Design: Emily Love

**ISBN**
978-1-63235-047-3 (hardcover)
978-1-63235-107-4 (paperback)
978-1-62143-088-9 (hosted ebook)

**Library of Congress Control Number: 2014937416**

Printed in the United States of America
Mankato, MN
June, 2014

# TABLE OF CONTENTS

# CHAPTER 1

# BIRTHDAY MAYHEM

**"She shoots . . . "**

Annie Roger leaped into the air and released the basketball in a beautiful arc. The ball hit the backboard, rattled off the front of the metal rim, and dropped through the hoop.

" . . . she scores!"

Sure, thirteen-year-old Annie was just shooting hoops in her driveway, but she envisioned herself making the game-winning shot, her teammates hoisting her into the air as she held up a gigantic trophy.

"The crowd goes wild! Ahhh!"

The ball bounced lazily back to her, and she scooped it off the asphalt. The ball—a bit lopsided, its bumps worn away with time and use—once belonged to her dad when he was her age. It was now Annie's most prized possession.

From inside the house, Annie heard the screeching of nine-year-old girls. Annie's sister, Olivia, was having a birthday party. Shooting hoops was Annie's way of getting away from the madness.

As she dribbled the ball on the driveway with one hand, Annie texted her friends with the other.

*Rescue me. Let's shoot hoops.*

She pocketed her phone and then shot the ball. It landed short, bouncing off the rim and ricocheting back toward her. Annie snatched it up and dribbled in for a layup.

She'd been playing for some time, and as much as she didn't want to brave the party inside, she needed a drink of water.

The side door was barely open an inch before Annie heard her sister shrieking, "I can't believe it! My very own Fabulous Princess Pony!"

Annie clapped her hands over her ears and tried hard to shut out the sound of sugar-powered nine-year-olds gathered in the living room. Olivia jumped up and down in the middle of the frenzy. She wore a purple dress with a ruffled tutu and a plastic tiara. She hugged a toy in a pink box.

"It's just what I wanted!" Olivia screamed. "Thanks, Mom! Thanks, Dad!"

"You're welcome, sweetie," Annie's mom said. She smiled, but Annie could tell her mom was super tired. She'd spent a lot of time preparing for the party. It looked like a birthday monster had thrown up all over their living room. Balloons. Signs. Confetti. Even a piñata shaped like one of the ponies that the girls were screaming about.

*Wow,* Annie thought. *If their screeching gets any louder, the windows are going to shatter.*

Annie poured herself a glass of water from the pitcher in the fridge. Then she walked into the living room, snatched up the remote, and turned on the TV. She rifled quickly through the channels, ending on a sports station broadcasting an NBA basketball game. The Los Angeles Lakers were playing the Miami Heat. It was in the fourth quarter, and the Lakers were up by three.

"Sweet!" Annie said. She cranked up the volume to drown out the sound of the squealing girls.

"Ahem." Her dad loudly cleared his throat. His hands were on his hips, and a stern look was carved into his face.

"Uh, yeah?" Annie tried to sound like everything was okay.

"Please turn the TV off."

"Dad, it's Lakers-Heat," Annie protested. "There's only three minutes left!"

"Your sister is having a birthday party," her dad said. "Please respect that."

"But basketball is way cooler than stupid princesses and ponies and stuff."

"Annie." The way her dad said her name, Annie knew he wasn't in the mood to argue. He looked almost as tired as her mom.

Annoyed, Annie clicked the TV off. As she did, there was a knock on the side door. She saw Ben Mason's face peering in the window. Of course Ben would get to her house first. He only lived across the street.

Annie hurried over, grabbed the basketball off the floor, and swung open the door.

"Hey!" Ben said. "I'm here for the rescue mission."

"Great timing," she said as her sister's friends began to squeal some more.

Once outside, Annie bounce-passed the ball to Ben. He dribbled up the drive while Annie played a loose defense. He leaped into the air, taking a jump shot. Annie threw her arm up to try to block it. She missed, and Ben's shot swished through the hoop.

They decided to play a game of HORSE. Annie dominated, draining shots from every angle of the driveway.

As Ben was attempting a hook shot, hoping not to get an "E" and therefore sealing Annie's victory, her mom poked her head out of the door. "We're singing and blowing out candles," she said. "If you want cake, I suggest you come inside now. You too, Ben."

"Did someone say cake?" Logan Parrish brought his bike to a screeching stop beside Ben. "I could have sworn I heard the word cake." He sniffed the air like a cartoon dog.

Gabe Santiago, the last of Annie's trio of friends, pedaled up the drive behind Logan. "*Hola*, guys!"

"Hey, Gabe," Annie and Ben said.

"So why do you need rescuing, Annie?" Gabe asked.

Annie tossed a thumb over her shoulder. "My sister's friends are all here for her birthday party. It's like a teakettle convention in there. I was hoping you guys wanted to go to Grover Park to play some b-ball. What do you say?"

Gabe nodded. "Yeah, of course."

Ben added, "Sounds like fun."

Logan looked concerned. "We're eating cake first, though, right?"

# CHAPTER 2

# A FRIENDLY GAME

**After scarfing down slices of chocolate cake and washing them down with fruit punch, the four friends ducked out of the party.** They rode their bikes through the town Grover Lake. Annie led the way. She cruised along sidewalks and streets with her basketball tucked under one arm.

In the middle of the town, there was a huge park with a duck pond, two baseball fields, a large pavilion for barbequing, and the biggest playground Annie had ever seen.

The park also had a full basketball court, complete with painted lines marking off half-court, the free throw lines, and the three-point circles. It was the best court in town, and it was Annie's favorite place to play.

She crossed her fingers that the court would be empty. As they rode up, she breathed a sigh of relief. No one was playing.

It was all theirs.

"All right, half-court, two on two," Annie said, leaping off her bike and bounding over to the court.

They split up, Ben and Gabe on one team, Annie and Logan on the other. Annie took the ball at the top of the key.

"First team to twenty," she said, passing the ball to Ben, who defended her. He checked it, and passed it back.

Even though Ben was taller than Annie, she was quicker and could easily out-maneuver him. She dribbled left, broke away, and sunk a jump shot from the corner.

"Two points! Count it!" she cheered.

"Lucky shot," Ben grumbled.

It wasn't, though. Annie was the best player on the court. She had a great eye and better instincts. She knew when to shoot and when to pass over to Logan, whose height difference against the squat Gabe was almost laughable. Thankfully, they never took their games too seriously. Playing basketball with her friends was always fun for Annie.

Annie and Logan easily took a ten-point lead against the other two boys, and they never looked back.

As Annie sunk a fade-away jumper from the free throw line for the game-winning points, she spied out of the corner of her eye four boys walking over to the court.

In the lead was a rail-thin boy their age with spiky brown hair. His name was Micah Nelson. He lived and went to school on the west side of Grover Lake, unlike Annie and the guys, who lived on the east side. Micah was really good pals with a boy named Jacob Fuller. Annie and her friends were not big fans of Jacob Fuller, who played baseball for their crosstown rivals, the West Grover Lake Fighting Hornets.

"Hey, guys," Micah said, a sneer flitting across his face.

"'Sup," Logan said. The others nodded but said nothing.

"Mind if we share the court?" Micah pointed at the other hoop. One of his friends, a tall but lean boy, dribbled a basketball.

Annie shrugged. "Go ahead."

The kids from West Grover Lake started shooting baskets on their side of the court while Annie and her friends switched teams for a second game. This time, Gabe was Annie's partner.

The more they played, though, the more Annie became distracted by the guys on the other end of the court. At first, she thought their offhand insults were about each other. As time passed, though, she realized they were talking about her.

"No way a girl can play as well as a boy," she heard Micah say.

"They're just not as strong," another kid said. "Not as tall. Not as fast. Am I right?"

"Oh, totally," said the tall kid. "She should stick to girly things, like Fabulous Princess Ponies."

"Do you think they give trophies out for shopping?" Micah asked.

They all laughed at this snide comment.

Annie wasn't the only one who heard them. Just as Logan was about to shoot a three-pointer, he pulled the ball down and turned to the West Grover Lake kids.

"Hey, man," he said. "Knock it off."

"What?" Micah threw his arms up questioningly.

"Keep your comments to yourself."

Micah laughed. "So what? You think she could beat me at basketball?"

"I don't *think* she can, dude. I *know*."

"Wanna bet?"

Micah and Logan were stepping closer and closer to one another. Logan had a habit of being a bit of a hothead. He was never one to back down from a challenge.

"Hey, cool it," Annie said. She placed her hands on Logan's chest and gently pushed him back.

"Yeah," Micah said. "I didn't think so. You're all talk."

Annie stopped. She'd had enough. Logan was right. This guy was a jerk. She turned and said, "Oh, really? All talk? You're on."

Micah was taken aback. "Really?"

"Really." Annie held out her hands, and Ben tossed her the ball. She smiled and said, "Bring it."

# CHAPTER 3

# SORE LOSERS

**"I'll try to go easy on you, okay?" Micah said as he walked over to the top of the key.**

"Just check the ball," Annie said. She had no intention of telling Micah and his cohorts that she was the starting point guard for her middle school team and that she was on track to play varsity by the time she was a freshman in high school.

They used Annie's lucky ball for the game. She passed it hard into Micah's chest. He passed it back just as hard.

"First team to twenty wins," Logan said.

"Sounds good," said the tall kid on Micah's team, whose name turned out to be Brett. He guarded Logan.

Annie dribbled the ball for a bit as the other guys ran around, trying to get open. They didn't have any special plays, like they did on her school team, but her friends had a few tricks. Logan ran up to Micah and set a pick, planting his feet and puffing out his chest. Annie used the pick, dribbled left around both boys, and drained a jump shot.

"Two-nothing," she said as Micah took the ball.

Micah was fast, but he wasn't the best ball handler. He passed the ball over to Brett, who stood in the paint—the rectangular area directly in front of the hoop. Brett's hook shot bounced off the rim.

Micah came down with the rebound. As he dribbled the ball back toward the top, Annie reached in, swatting it away from him.

"Great steal, Annie!" Ben shouted as she scooped up the ball and fed it down to Gabe.

Gabe made a routine layup.

"Four-zip," Logan said. "Uh-oh. It's not looking good, Micah."

Micah cursed under his breath.

Annie outplayed Micah the entire game, and his frustration was obvious. Once, when Annie lined up for a three-point shot, he swung his arm down, hit her hand, and batted the ball away.

"Foul!" Logan shouted, pointing at Micah and stopping play.

"What are you talking about?" Micah countered. "That was all ball. Totally clean!"

"Clean?" Logan laughed. "That was about as clean as a garbage dump, dude."

"Let it go, Logan," Annie said.

Micah and his team kept themselves in the game, thanks to Brett's rebounding and height. Both teams played hard. Soon, Annie was wiping sweat from her brow with her shirtsleeve.

With the score 18–14 in their favor, Annie took the ball at the top of the key. "Game point," she said to Micah.

"Pfft! No way I'm getting beat by a girl," Micah muttered back.

His constant attacks had finally taken their toll. Annie was furious. She wanted nothing more than to sink the winning shot, laugh in Micah's face, and leave the court victorious.

Annie played more aggressively than usual. She faked left and drove right. Logan was open in the corner, and she quickly dished the ball to him. He lined up a shot, but Brett waved his long arms in Logan's face, so he pulled the ball back down.

Annie ran to a gap in the defense, right by the free throw line. She clapped her hands. "Logan! Here!" He bounced the ball right to her.

Annie turned, lined up the shot—

*Smack!*

Micah knocked the ball away, hard. It sailed off the court and toward the winding street that curved around the park. Annie was forced backward, and she fell painfully.

"Dude!" Logan shouted. He ran at Micah, whose friends quickly swarmed around him. Gabe and Ben joined Logan.

Annie didn't care about that, though. "Where's my ball?!" She looked around, finally spying the ball as it rolled out into the street.

As it did, a large, green delivery truck drove past. The ball skipped under the truck's front wheels. Annie waited for it to appear again at the truck's rear, praying it would escape unscathed.

*POP!*

All hope burst as she heard the ball explode under the force of the truck's tires.

# CHAPTER 4

# DEFLATED

**"This is the worst day ever," Annie muttered.**
She and her friends were sitting in a booth at the Lake Diner, a small restaurant they frequented. The diner was known for its milk shakes and had, as Logan put it, "the greatest bacon cheeseburger in the history of the world, even going back as far the cavemen and their mammoth burgers or dinosaur burgers or whatever they ate back then."

Annie set the basketball, which was now nothing more than a deflated, flattened mass, on the table. All four kids stared at it. No one said a word. Annie tried hard to fight back tears. She didn't like to cry, and she hated that she was so close to doing it now, in front of her friends.

Their waitress, an older woman with a bundle of energy and wispy white hair that was twirled and hidden inside a handkerchief on her head, walked over to their booth. Her name tag said ROSA, but none of the kids needed to read it to know the woman. Rosa was Gabe's grandmother. She had been working at the Lake Diner all their lives.

"*Hola*, gang," she said with a thick accent. Then she saw the ball, and her nose wrinkled. "What is that?"

"It's Annie's basketball," Gabe told her.

"Oh. Shouldn't it be, you know . . . " She drew a circle with one hand. " . . . round?"

"It was run over by a truck," Annie said quietly. She picked at the ball's burst seam with one finger.

"Sorry to hear that, sweetheart," Rosa said. "Let me bring you all some milk shakes."

"Thanks, *abuelita*," Gabe said.

They sat staring at the deflated ball, not knowing what to say. Around them, the diner buzzed with activity. It was the middle of the afternoon, but somehow, no matter the hour, the Lake Diner was always busy.

Rosa brought them more than just milk shakes. She set a giant red basket overflowing with piping-hot french fries in the center of the table.

"Someone made a mistake with their order," she said with a wink.

The boys ate like they'd never seen food before. Logan squirted a mountain of ketchup onto a small plate and drowned his fries in it. Gabe ate four at a time. And when he thought no one was watching, Ben dipped his fries into his vanilla milk shake.

Annie couldn't eat, though. She kept thinking about her basketball. And about how Micah and his friends had teased her. They even laughed when she ran into the street after her squashed ball.

"You okay, Annie?" Ben asked between mouthfuls.

He and Annie had always been close. He had a knack for telling when she was upset.

However, it didn't take intuition to know how she was feeling right now.

"No," she answered. "I don't usually care what other kids think. But Micah really got to me today."

"They're just dumb boys," Gabe said.

"Yeah, don't listen to them," Logan said. "Your actions speak volumes. And you proved to them that you're just as good as they are."

"Better," Ben said, chewing on a fry.

"Exactly." Logan picked up the flattened ball. "Now, next time you see Rosa, tell her I'm going to need some syrup to eat this pancake."

Despite feeling down, Annie laughed at Logan's joke.

They finished their milk shakes and left a mound of change and crumpled bills on the table. Rosa gave Gabe a big hug, and the friends headed for the door.

A giant corkboard was hung on the wall next to the door. Flyers were tacked up all over it, from people looking for roommates to cheap piano lessons to class schedules for the local community center. A bright yellow flyer in the middle of the board was what grabbed Annie's attention.

She stopped in her tracks.

"Check it out," she said. The boys leaned in close.

On the flyer was an illustration of a basketball swishing through a hoop. Jagged lines, like an explosion, radiated out from it. In bold letters above the hoop, it read:

*3RD ANNUAL CITYWIDE 5-ON-5 BASKETBALL TOURNEY!! ALL AGE BRACKETS!! SIGN UP NOW!!* And in smaller print at the bottom of the sheet: *Register your team at one of our sponsors: Fritz's Barbershop, Fuller Fridges & More, Sal's Used Sporting Goods, and Lowell Hardware!*

"Hey, guys," Annie said. "We should totally sign up."

Ben nodded. "Yeah. What better way to show Micah how awesome at basketball you are than to enter this tourney and win?"

"Fuller Fridges?" Logan said. "That's Jacob Fuller's dad's business. How much do you want to bet he and Micah are on a team already?"

"That settles it," Annie said. "Tomorrow, I'm going to Sal's to sign us up."

# CHAPTER 5

# GIRL POWER

**Sal's didn't open until noon on Sundays, so Annie spent the morning in her pajamas watching *SportsCenter* on the small TV in her bedroom.** As lunchtime approached, she changed into jeans and a hoodie, told her parents where she was going, and raced out the door.

Sal's Used Sporting Goods shop was located in an older section of Grover Lake that consisted of brick and stone buildings. Annie could get there in her sleep. She loved Sal's and had a feeling there would be more to her trip than simply signing up for a basketball tournament.

She leaned her bike under the store's familiar orange awning and entered the shop.

Usually, Sal was waiting with an exuberant greeting. Not this time. The store was quiet and in more disarray than usual. A sign resting against the cluttered front glass display case said SALE! in big red letters.

"Sal?"

Annie walked over to the display case. Next to the register was the same flyer as the one at the Lake Diner. Next to it was taped a sign-up sheet. The top half was already filled with names.

She found a pen and began to fill in the appropriate information. When she reached the space labeled "Team Name," though, she paused.

"Well, well, well. It's about time you joined the tournament, Miss Roger." Sal Horton, a barrel-chested man with a wide smile, stood in the doorway behind the counter, which led to the store's basement. He held an armload of badminton racquets.

"Hey, Sal!" Annie said. "Whatcha doing?"

Sal set the wooden racquets on the counter with a clatter.

"Cleaning out the basement by having a big sale," he said. "You think it's cluttered up here? That's nothing compared with what's down there." Sal leaned forward on the counter and continued, saying cryptically, "Speaking of the basement, I found something in storage that I expect you'll find *very* interesting."

Annie smiled. *Knew it.*

Sal turned and picked something up off the floor. He set it on the counter between them.

It was a basketball, old and faded, with orange and white stripes. There was a logo of a basketball with a tail curling behind it and the word COMETS below it.

*It's like he already knew my basketball had been flattened,* Annie thought.

Sal explained. "This ball was used by the very first team to win the Women's National Basketball Association championship, the Houston Comets."

Annie knew about the Comets. They were one of the eight teams in the league when it started, but they weren't around anymore.

"This is amazing, Sal," Annie said, picking up the ball and sliding it around in her hands. "My favorite basketball was run over by a truck yesterday."

"Oh my," Sal said.

"Yeah. Some boy named Micah knocked it into the street. He was making fun of me, saying that girls can't play basketball with boys."

"Well, then clearly this boy has not heard of Nancy Lieberman."

"Who?" Surprisingly, Annie wasn't familiar with the name, either.

Sal rummaged behind the counter, retrieved a book, and flipped through its pages until he came to a photo of a woman. She was blonde and muscular, driving down a basketball court. "Lieberman was a member of the *first* United States women's Olympic basketball team, back in 1976. Then she became the first woman to play in a *men's* professional basketball league."

"She did?"

"Yep. The United States Basketball League."

"Whoa," Annie said.

"You see, strong women have been playing basketball for more than a hundred years. Forget what that boy said. Keep your chin up."

"Thanks, Sal."

Annie pushed the ball back across the counter.

"Oh no," Sal said. "That's for you. Use it. Otherwise it'll just be collecting dust."

"You're the best, Sal." Annie scooped up the ball. She couldn't wait to call the guys.

She was nearly to the door when Sal called out to her. She spun around to see him tapping on the sign-up sheet. "Your team needs a name," he said.

Annie smiled. She'd just thought of the perfect one.

# CHAPTER 6

# PRACTICE MAKES PERFECT

**"Annie's Comets?"** Ben's face was scrunched up in confusion.

"Yep. That's our team name." Annie dribbled the ball between her legs. She still couldn't believe she owned a basketball used by a championship WNBA team. It felt wrong to use the ball, but that was why Sal had given it to her.

Later that afternoon, she and the guys were hanging out at the Grover Park basketball court. It was their first official practice for the tournament.

"Why the Comets?" Logan asked.

Annie bounced him the ball. "Check the logo. The Houston Comets were the WNBA champions the league's first four years."

"Cool." Logan passed the ball back to her. Annie launched a three-point shot.

*Swish!*

Nothing but net.

She knew there was no such thing as magic. But man, that basketball was about as close as it got.

They shot free throws to determine teams for a two-on-two game, and Annie and

Ben wound up together. Annie took the ball at the key, and Logan checked it before tossing it back to her.

She dribbled through her legs and drove to her right. Ben snuck up and set a pick on Logan, and Annie quickly ran around them.

"Switch!" Gabe called, now covering Annie. She stopped, pulled up, and looked to shoot. Her head fake worked, as Gabe leaped into the air. As he came down, off balance, Annie shot an easy jumper off the backboard.

"Two points," she said, holding up her index and middle fingers. "Count it."

Logan took the ball up top, and Annie crouched in her defensive stance. She kept her eyes on his waist. Following a player's head or eye movements could get you in trouble, but their hips never lied.

Logan dribbled to his right, and Annie was on him. When he passed the ball to Gabe, she swatted it away. Ben scooped it up, brought it to the key, and found Annie in the paint. She looked to shoot, was covered by both boys, and rocketed a pass out to Ben.

He drained the jump shot.

"Uh-oh," Annie said. "Looks like you're in trouble, boys."

They played to twenty, and even though Annie and Ben got off to a hot start, Gabe and Logan made them work for the win. Annie nailed a three-pointer from the corner to seal the victory. She held her follow-through—arm up in the air, hand curled down at the wrist— until long after the shot had been drained.

"That's game!" Ben shouted, giving her a high five.

They took a break after the game, grabbing a drink from a water fountain by the park's pavilion.

On the walk back to the court, a puzzled Gabe asked, "So, um, about our team. Don't we need five people to play?"

Annie nodded. "Yep. Actually, there's our fifth player now." She pointed across the park, where a tall, lanky boy pedaled his bike furiously toward them.

"Hey!" Ben said. "It's Ty!"

Tyler Murphy was one of the group's classmates. He played with all of them on their baseball team, the East Grover Lake Grizzlies. Ty was the team's first baseman, and he played center for the school's basketball team. He was a perfect fit for their group. Annie had called him after leaving Sal's, and he had gladly accepted her invitation to be on their team.

"Hey, guys!" Ty dismounted his bike and joined them on the court.

"Oh man," Logan said, slapping Ty a high five, "no one's gonna mess with us with you throwing elbows under the hoop."

"You can slam-dunk, can't you?" the short Gabe asked.

Ty smiled.

Gabe shook his head. "I'm so jealous."

"Okay," Annie said, becoming all business. "If we're gonna crush Micah's team, we're gonna need a few plays that up our game. You guys have heard of the motion offense, right?"

The boys nodded. They all played on school teams and had run this simple but effective play before.

"Good," Annie said. "Let's do it."

Annie knew the key to motion offense was constant movement. All five players spaced themselves at various spots on the court. Annie played point guard at the top of the key. Gabe was their small forward to her left, Ben the shooting guard on her right. Ty and Logan, the team's two tallest members, were down near the hoop. Logan was the power forward, and Tyler their center.

They ran the basics of motion offense until it was smooth. Then Annie shouted, "Okay! Give and go!"

She passed the ball to Gabe and then darted toward the hoop. He fed the ball back to her. Instead of shooting a layup, though, Annie slid the ball across to Logan, who backed up to the three-point line and drained the shot.

"Nice one!" Ben cheered.

Back at the top, Annie said, "Okay, let's try a pick and roll!"

Ty dashed up to her and pretended to block an imaginary defender. Annie dribbled the ball around him. Then Ty peeled down toward the hoop. Annie lobbed the ball up to him. He caught it and, without dribbling, leaped up and laid the ball right in. His jump was so high and his reach so long that Ty's fingers were above the metal rim.

They practiced like this for another hour, until they were all sweating and in need of another water break.

Excitement fluttered in Annie's stomach. Annie's Comets had a real shot of winning the tournament, and she couldn't wait to take the court.

# CHAPTER 7

# ANOTHER GIFT FROM SAL

**On Friday, the day before the basketball tournament, Annie returned home from school to find a note from her mom on the kitchen counter.** It read: *Sal called. He wants you and your friends to stop by the store. Be home for dinner.*

Sal's sale was in full swing. A number of patrons wandered through the packed aisles.

Sal was at his usual spot behind the counter. A cardboard box rested in front of him.

"Greetings, Annie's Comets!"

Nearly in unison, Annie and the guys said "Hey, Sal!" They huddled around the counter before him.

"I have something that I wanted to give you." Sal reached into the box and withdrew a white jersey. He held it out in both hands so they could see the shirt's design. In blue lettering on the back, it read: *SAL'S SPORTS!* Below that was a comical illustration of Sal's smiling face.

"I had them made a long time ago," Sal explained. "I thought your team might need a sponsor."

"These are awesome, Sal," Annie said.

The boys agreed.

They rummaged through the box of matching shirts until they each found the correct size. Then they slid their new jerseys on over their T-shirts.

Logan puffed out his chest and put his fists on his hips. "How do we look?"

Annie laughed. "Like a team," she proudly proclaimed.

Annie wore her white jersey to bed that evening. It smelled a bit musty and old, and her mother offered to wash it for her, but Annie refused. She feared washing the shirt might take its magic away.

She barely slept. When the alarm clock on her phone began to chirp and the sun began to creep in through the slats of her windows, Annie was already awake and raring to go.

Her parents and sister were sitting at the dining room table enjoying a peaceful breakfast when Annie came bounding down the steps. Her sneakers and gear were packed in a red equipment bag slung over her shoulder. Annie inhaled her breakfast so fast she wasn't sure if she chewed her food or not.

Then, before the rest of her family could react, Annie walked toward the front door and shouted, "Come on, people! Get a move on. I've got a tournament to win!"

# CHAPTER 8

# LET THE GAMES BEGIN!

**The tournament was held at the Grover Lake Community Center, an old building downtown.** The parking lot was packed with cars. It seemed most of Grover Lake had turned out for the competition.

Annie led her parents and sister, who carried her birthday pony in the crook of one arm and wore a tiara on her head, into the building.

In the middle of the community center was an enormous gymnasium with three basketball courts lined up next to one another. Sunlight filtered through windows high in the gym, casting rays of light on the dark hardwood floor.

A number of kids were already on the courts. Their sneakers squeaked, and the thunder of dribbling basketballs echoed off the walls.

A table was set up near the gym's door. A woman helping teams sign in was seated behind it. On the wall, large posters displayed the tournament's various brackets.

Annie was scanning their age group's bracket when she heard Ben say, "Mornin', captain!"

She turned and saw the rest of her team, all sporting their white jerseys. "Looking good, guys," Annie said.

There were eight teams in their age bracket. That meant they needed to win two games in order to play in the championship. Annie found their name on the left side of the bracket. "Annie's Comets versus Nothin' But Net," she said. "We play in thirty minutes."

"Look," Logan said, pointing to the right side of the bracket. "Fuller's Fiends. That's Micah and Jacob's team."

"If they're on that side, then the only chance we'll play them would be in the championship," Gabe said.

"Perfect." Annie smiled devilishly.

They signed in with the tournament organizers. "You're on court number three," the woman told them.

Annie led the way. She spied Micah, Brett, and the towering Jacob Fuller standing near court one. Micah curled his lip in a smug smile.

As Annie sat on the sideline bench and laced up her shoes, she looked around at the teams playing. She saw other girls practicing and warming up, but they—and Annie—were definitely in the minority.

After a brief warm-up period, one of the referees for their game gathered the teams at mid court. Annie recognized a few of the Nets' players. They went to the other middle school in Grover Lake and were classmates with Micah.

"Rules are simple," the ref said. "Ten-minute halves, two time-outs per team, all other standard basketball rules apply. Got it?"

They all nodded.

Each team was also expected to bring a backup basketball to be used if needed. Annie brought her Comets ball.

Ty and the Nets' center lined up for the tip-off.

The referee blew the whistle and threw the ball high into the air.

Ty swatted it back to Annie.

She dribbled up the court and then dished the ball off to Ben, who quickly fed Ty inside. The center for the Nets was tall, but Ty easily shot over the kid's outstretched arm.

His shot banked off the backboard and went in.

The Nets weren't much competition. Their point guard had a habit of dribbling the ball far away from his body, and Annie stole it from him easily and often. She fed passes through openings in the defense and hit fade-away jump shots like no one was covering her.

She'd brought her A game for sure.

When the buzzer sounded at the end of the game, Annie's Comets won by the score 42–24.

They had about forty-five minutes to rest before their next game. As they grabbed some water, Annie saw Micah's team playing on the first court. The red scoreboard at mid court showed they were obliterating their opponents.

Annie's Comets faced a bigger challenge in their second game. They played the Double Dribblers, a team that included some of their schoolmates. The Dribblers' point guard was a boy named Grayson, who was very speedy. Gray played point guard for the East Grover Lake Middle School team. Annie had to work extra hard on maintaining ball control, because Gray was known for his stealing abilities.

Annie had a terrible game. She turned the ball over a number of times and only hit a small percentage of her jumpers. It didn't help that she caught Micah and the rest of his team watching their game from the bleachers. That made her feel nervous.

"Go Double Dribblers!" Micah yelled, whistling through his fingers.

Annie kicked herself for letting the bully get in her head.

Thankfully, Ben got a hot hand in the second half of the game. He drained four three-pointers in a row. The Comets went up by two, and though Grayson had a chance to tie the game with a last-second shot, Annie got her hand on the ball and tipped it off course.

It ricocheted off the side of the rim and fell flat.

The Comets were playing in the championship game!

# CHAPTER 9

# REMATCH

**It was just as Annie had hoped.** They were playing in the championship against Micah and his team. As they all walked out to mid court, Annie looked around. Their game had attracted a number of people, and the bleachers were packed. She spied her family halfway up, clapping and cheering.

"Fancy meeting you here," she said to Micah as they prepared for tip-off.

He sneered at her.

Despite Ty's height, Jacob Fuller had him beat by a couple of inches. Fuller won the tip-off easily, swatting the ball into Micah's hands. Micah raced up the court, challenging Annie right away. He faked left and dribbled right. Annie tried to keep her eyes on his midsection, but her feet tangled up beneath her and she went down.

Micah scored easily.

As he jogged back on defense, Micah asked, "You sure you still want to play against us?"

Annie hurried to her feet and said nothing.

She couldn't seem to get into a rhythm. Micah had her flustered. He easily stole the ball from her, and when she picked up her dribble too soon, he guarded her so close she could hardly pass the ball.

The Fiends were also playing dirty. Down in the paint, Jacob Fuller threw elbows left and right. The refs called him for a couple of fouls, but Ty was having a tough time getting the ball.

Brett, on the other hand, sank every three-pointer he shot, despite Logan's excellent defense.

By the time the buzzer sounded at the end of the first half, the Fiends were up 26–14.

Annie and the guys sat huddled on the bench, drinking from water bottles and sweating profusely.

"We need to be more aggressive," Annie said. "Let's show these guys what we're made of!"

She held her hand out, palm down. The others stacked theirs on top.

"One, two, three . . . COMETS!" they all shouted.

Annie tightened up her ballhandling in the second half, coming out strong and hitting a fade-away jumper from the corner. The second time she came up the court, though, Micah slammed into her, swatting the ball away.

The ref blew the whistle and called him for a personal foul.

The ball had bounced out of bounds and had somehow skirted beneath the wooden bleachers and out of sight.

Jogging to the sidelines, the ref grabbed the first ball he found and passed it to Annie for the inbound pass.

It was her WNBA Comets ball.

Suddenly, Micah was yelling at the ref and pointing to her ball. "Hey, that ball's not legal. It's a girl's ball."

The ref turned to Annie. "Can I see that?"

She wasn't sure what was going on but handed it to him.

The ref spun it around in his hands until he came across the Comet's logo. "He's right," the ref said. "WNBA balls are slightly smaller than NBA balls, and that's what we use for the middle schools boys age bracket."

"Can you believe that?" Micah sneered in her direction. "Next she'll probably want us to play with dolls."

The ref went and grabbed another legal-sized basketball.

Not being able to use her ball didn't upset Annie, but she was furious at Micah's comment. She wanted to beat him, now more than ever. Renewed determination swelled in her chest. She passed the ball in to Ben, who bounced it back to her. As she hit the top of the key, Logan dashed up and set a great pick on Micah. Annie rolled right, stopped, and fired a jump shot.

*Swish!*

"Great shot, Annie!" she heard her dad cheer.

The Comets went on a streak, using their new aggression, fighting and clawing to get back in the game. On defense, Logan was able to steal the ball off Brett. He saw Ty streaking down the court and threw it, one-handed, over everyone's head. Ty caught it, jumped up, and slam-dunked the ball.

The crowd went nuts.

Now it was Annie's turn to have Micah back on his heels. She dribbled circles around him. On defense, she caused a number of turnovers, including one where Micah dribbled the ball off his foot.

"I think you're confusing basketball with soccer, dude," Logan joked as he jogged past an embarrassed Micah.

The Comets fought hard, but with only one minute left in the game, Fuller's Fiends still held on to the lead by four points, 42–38.

Time was running out for Annie's Comets.

# CHAPTER 10

# A CHAMPION IS CROWNED

**Annie checked the clock.**

*Forty-five seconds.*

She brought the ball up the court, dished to Gabe, and broke for the hoop. Gabe faked left and then bounce-passed back to Annie. She went up with her right hand and took the shot. It rattled off the backboard, swirled around the rim . . . and went in!

"Back on defense!" Ben shouted.

Annie darted back. Her drive to win was stronger than ever. Micah took the inbound pass and dribbled toward half-court. He was stalling, trying to run out the clock.

Annie glanced over.

Thirty seconds left.

Micah passed the ball to Jacob before the ref could call him for a five-second violation. Jacob faked a shot, but Ty was right in his face, so he passed the ball back to Micah—and Annie was there to knock it away.

She dashed after the loose ball. The Comets needed to get at least two points so they could tie up the game and send it to overtime. Annie scooped up the ball just before it sailed out of bounds. She dribbled down the sideline on a breakaway, past the cheering, frenzied crowd. She saw her parents clapping, and Olivia jumping up and down.

Micah came at her from the opposite side of the court. He was racing her to the hoop, trying to cut off her chance at an easy layup.

It was going to be close.

Annie looked to dish the ball, but she was on her own. The crowd counted down. "Five . . . four . . . three . . . "

Annie went up for a left-handed layup.

Micah leaped up, but mistimed his jump. As the ball rolled off Annie's fingertips, he swatted at her, hitting her square on the arm, knocking her to the wooden floor.

The crowd gasped.

The referee blew his whistle just as the buzzer sounded.

Annie looked up at the hoop. The ball rolled around, seeming to balance itself on the rim, as if deciding whether or not to fall.

The crowd was so quiet Annie could practically hear her heart thudding in her chest.

The ball wavered . . . and fell through the net!

"The basket counts!" the ref shouted. "Foul! One free throw!"

With the score tied, Annie had a chance to win it all.

*No pressure*, she thought.

She stepped up to the free throw line and took a deep, calming breath. She tried to shut out the commotion, tried not to pay attention to Micah and Jacob Fuller muttering things about her as she waited for the ref to pass her the ball.

He did, and Annie dribbled a couple of times. She let out another breath and looked down at the ball in her hands.

*Time to prove Micah wrong about girls,* she thought.

She raised the ball overhead, leaned back, aimed, and shot.

The ball moved as if in slow motion. It rotated and arced high, hit the front of the rim, bounced off the backboard . . .

. . . and went in.

"Yes!" Annie leaped into the air as the crowd burst into frenzied cheers. Ben and Logan and Gabe and Ty swarmed her, picked her up, and lifted her high into the air.

Annie looked down at Micah and saw him hanging his head and walking off the court. She wanted so very much to flaunt her victory. But suddenly, she realized that if she did, she'd be no better than Micah.

"Let me down," she ordered the guys.

They did.

Annie jogged over to Micah. "Hey," she said.

He stopped and turned around. "What do you want?"

Annie held out her hand. "Good game," she said. "You guys played really well."

Micah stared at her hand, eyeing her up like he expected her to pull a prank on him. Hesitant, he offered his hand.

They shook. "Yeah," Micah muttered. "Yeah, you too. Good game, Annie."

"And the winners from the twelve-to fourteen-year-old bracket," said the announcer over a loudspeaker, "Annie's Comets, sponsored by Sal's Used Sporting Goods."

The crowd clapped and cheered as Annie, Ben, Gabe, Logan, and Ty stepped to center court. Annie had her lucky basketball tucked under one arm.

The organizers of the tournament handed each of them a small trophy. It was lightweight, with a statue of a basketball player shooting a layup on top. The tournament's name and date were etched on the trophy's base.

Annie held the trophy aloft. Today, she had proven herself. She was proud of her friends, and excited to share this victory with them. In the back of the crowd, she